THE CHILD

SANTAS LITTLE HELPER

EMILY MUSGROVE

Little Molly Buttons and her family loved Christmas. Their little cottage that sat on top of a BIG hill was always decorated both inside and out at Christmas time. It had become The Buttons festive tradition.

During the days before Christmas little Molly would help her mum to make all kinds of Christmas treats. Molly especially liked helping her mum to make mince pies for Christmas. These were very special because some of the mince pies would be left for Santa along with a small glass of sherry and a saucer of milk and a carrot for his faithful reindeer, Rudolf and his friends.

Little Molly ALWAYS wrote Santa a THANK

YOU note and left it above the coal burning fire, letting him know that the sherry, mince pies, saucer of milk and carrots were waiting for him and his reindeer's on the old wooden table in the kitchen. They were purposely put there because Molly did not want Bobbles the dog or Buttercup the cat to eat them, and of course it was very important that the sherry not get too hot before Santa had a chance to drink it, and the milk did not curdle before Rudolf and the other reindeer's drank it.

The night before Christmas, Molly helped her mum and dad put the presents under the Christmas tree and then she went outside with Bobbles and Buttercup to play in the snow. Molly made a snow angel and tried to build a snowman, but the snow would not stick together properly. Molly came in the house after playing in the snow, and she ate her supper while watching television with her mum and dad before getting into her pink pyjamas. Then, excitedly Molly hung her Christmas stocking on the fireplace mantle and went upstairs to get

ready for bed and
wait for Santa
coming.

Once her teeth had
been brushed and
her face washed,
Molly went to her
bedroom and jumped
straight into bed! Her
dad came in and read
her a Christmas story
about a little
snowman called
Frosty.

"Is it still snowing?"
asked Molly just
before her dad got

the chance to turn out the light.

Dad looked out of the window and answered, "Yes, if it keeps up, there could be a lot more snow before morning."

"Do you think Santa Claus can still get here?" asked Molly, "You don't think that it will be snowing too hard for him to find us, daddy?"

"I am sure that Santa will not have any problems finding us,

Molly. After all, he has snow at the North Pole all year round." Her Dad said with a warming smile.

"I bet Santa and Rudolf practice a lot, don't they?" said Molly smiling back at her dad.

"I bet they do!" laughed her Dad, "Good night Molly - see you in the morning when

Santa's been with all your presents."

"Goodnight Daddy."

Molly's dad turned out her bedroom light and closed the door. Now, her bedroom room was in darkness except for the faint glow of the landing light that shone from beneath the door.

Molly closed her BIG blue eyes and drifted off to sleep. It was not long before she was dreaming of the wonderful presents that Santa Clause would bring her… Weeks ago Molly had sent Santa a long letter with some ideas. Her mum had told her that the list was too long and there was no way that Santa would be able to bring her everything on the list, especially with all the other good boys and girls around the world who deserved to receive their wonderful presents too.

"I know Santa Claus cannot bring me everything," Molly had said, "that is why I wrote:

Dear Santa Claus,

Here is my list of things that I would really like.

- *Teddy Bear*
- *Skipping Rope*
- *New pair of ice skates*
- *Nintendo DS*
- *Dolls House*

- *Hat and Scarf*

I know that the list is very long but if you could bring one or two things I would be really happy. I have tried to be good all year long. I know I was not always as good as I should have been but I did try. I was even good after Danny Bell made fun of my old scruffy skates that used to belong to my cousin Dorothy.

Thank you and Merry Xmas.
Love Molly Buttons

"I am glad that you understand that Santa cannot bring everything you want, but I am sure he will help to make this a good Christmas." said Mum.

"I love Christmas." said Molly.

"I know," answered Mum, "we all do."

For some reason, Molly awoke from her sleep just before her beside clock turned midnight. She did not know why she woke up so early but she did. She decided that maybe she was too excited about seeing what presents she was going to get her mum and dad and Santa Claus. She decided to get out of bed and see if Santa had come yet. There was something very exciting about seeing all of the stockings filled to the top with presents and the tree surrounded in colourful paper. Molly put on her pink slippers and quietly sneaked out of her bedroom and crept down the stairs because she did not want to wake up her mum and dad. As she rounded the corner to the living room, she was amazed. Molly caught Santa Claus and a little elf coming down the chimney!

"WOW!" exclaimed Molly, "SANTA CLAUS!"

"Little Molly Buttons," said Santa Claus, "what on earth are you doing out of bed at this time of night?"

"I am really sorry Santa," said Molly, "I could not sleep and decided to come and see if you had been yet."

"Do you promise not to tell anyone that you saw me?" asked Santa, "it is very important that what we do on Christmas Eve stay a secret." "I promise," said Molly.

"Santa, I really do not feel well," said the little Elf.

"How about you lie down on The Button's

couch for a few minutes while I get Molly's presents? Maybe you will feel better after a bit of rest."

"Okay, Santa," said the little Elf who did look an awful shade of green!

The little Elf lay down on the couch and covered himself with a blanket. Within a few minutes he was fast asleep and snoring his little head off!

Santa filled the stocking that hung beside the wood burning fire with a flick of his finger that pointed toward the large red Christmas sack and then another flick of his finger towards the stocking. The sack and the stocking seemed to understand the way that Santa's fingers worked before small wrapped packages flew from the big bag into the Christmas stocking. Then, Santa repeated what he had just done; only this time he flicked his finger at the sack and then the Christmas tree. Once again, packages flew out of the bag and arranged themselves around the tree. Only this time the packages were bigger.

"WOW MAGIC!" said Molly.

"Yes, special Christmas magic" said Santa "which is why it is important that you do not tell anyone what you saw tonight. I know that you are a good little girl, Molly, but there are some not very nice people who would enjoy seeing me stripped of my Christmas magic, because they would like to use it all up at once to get what they want."

"I promise not to tell," Molly said, "Santa, will your little Elf be okay?"

"Yes, Little Elf will be fine. I think he ate too many mince pies, and drank too much sherry, and then we flew so high in the sky that he is not feeling very well right now. I don't know if he likes heights either." Santa said rubbing his bald head. "But what really concerns me at this moment Molly, is that I am a little worried about getting the rest of the presents delivered though. I still have so many countries to visit with so many children and I would hate to disappoint anyone come morning," said Santa.

"I could help you," said Molly.

"I promise not to tell any of your secrets."

"Hmmmm… Do you think your Mum and Dad would mind if you came with me?" asked Santa.

"No, I think they would let me." said Molly.

"Okay… Well how about you go up and ask them? I wouldn't want them to wake up in the morning and have them find you gone missing and a Little Elf sleeping on their couch!" laughed Santa Claus.

"Okay." said Molly and she ran up the stairs and knocked on her Mum and Dad's bedroom door before going in. Molly quietly crept around to her Dad's side of the bed and whispered 'Dad... Dad... Are you awake?"

"I am now," said Dad "is everything okay? It's a little too early for you to open your presents."

"Dad, Santa came," said Molly, "and Little Elf isn't feeling very well because he ate too many mince pies and drank too much sherry, so he is going to stay here and rest on the couch, but Santa needs help to finish delivering his presents. He said that I could go and help him. Can I? Can I?"

"Where is Santa right now?" asked Dad climbing out of bed in his pyjamas. "Downstairs in our living room," answered Molly.

"I will be down in a minute. I would like to speak to Santa Claus before you go anywhere," replied Dad.

"Okay, but hurry, Dad, Santa Claus is very busy tonight. I don't want to keep him waiting. He is already worried about getting the rest of his presents delivered tonight."

"I won't be long," answered Dad, "just let me get dressed, please."

"Okay," said Molly as she hurried out of her Mum and Dad's bedroom and rushed back down the stairs to see Santa Claus.

"My Dad wants to talk to you," said Molly, "he will be here in a minute. He promised not to take long."

"I understand," said Santa, "your Dad needs to make sure that it is safe for you to come with me. It is not a usual request for a little girl to ask his father if she can go with Santa to deliver presents, and after all, if you come with me, you will be flying in the sky in a sleigh pulled by my faithful reindeer, Rudolf, you will be landing on snow-covered rooftops and then going down chimneys to help get all the presents be delivered to the good little boys and girls."

"What do bad boys and girls get for Christmas?" asked Molly, "is it really a lump of coal?"

"The lump of coal is a myth, Molly," said Santa, "to help boys and girls be good during the year. Most boys and girls are mostly good, with just some bad things sometimes. I give difficult boys and girls a special note from myself and Mrs. Claus along with a few things that they need like new mittens or a hat, sometimes a teddy bear or some roller-skates. Some of the difficult children just need something to do to keep them busy or someone to talk to. A teddy or a doll can be someone for a child to talk to. The naughty and nice list is not as easy to understand as the movies make it on television."

"WOW!" said Molly with a smile, "it is very nice that you try to help children be good."

"Well THANK YOU" answered Santa. Then, he and Molly ate the mince pies while they waited for her Dad to come downstairs. He appeared a few minutes later.

"Hello, Santa Claus," said Molly's Dad entering the living room.

"Ah, Timothy Buttons, it has been years!" said Santa Claus.

"You two know each other?" asked a rather puzzled and curious little Molly.

"Just from when I used to write my letters to Santa and he came down my chimney when I was a little boy. But this is our first meeting in person." Dad laughed.

"I am sure that Molly told you about Little Elf being ill. If you would allow Molly to help me deliver the rest of the presents, it would be very helpful to me." said Santa.

"But Molly is just an eight year old girl. She doesn't know anything about delivering presents especially in your line of work," said Molly's Dad.

"I promise to take good care of Molly and not let anything happen to her, if you will give permission for Molly to come with me. I have magic dust that will allow Molly to become an elf for this very important night Mr. Buttons. I don't want to rush you in your decision but I must be going. I am already concerned about delivering the rest of the gifts on time," said Santa Claus.

"She can go with you," said Molly's

Dad, "but Molly you must listen to everything that Santa Claus says. Do you understand?"

"Yes, Dad, I promise I will be on my best behaviour and be very helpful to Santa Claus," said Molly.

With those words, Santa Claus took his finger and waved it around Molly's head, sprinkling her with magical Christmas dust. When the dust encircled Molly, her pyjamas changed to a green Elf costume from the top of her head all the way down to her shiny shoes.

"Wow!" exclaimed Molly, "I am an elf now."

"Yes, you are, we will call you Molly the Elf. We must hurry, we have much work left to do and not much time to do it in," said Santa Claus. "Let me grab my sack and then you take my hand. We must go up the chimney and get back to the sledge and Rudolf."

Molly did as she was told and took Santa's hand and then he whispered to the blazing fire in the fireplace and the next thing Molly and Sana were flying up to the chimney where Rudolf and the other reindeer's awaited them on the snow covered roof.

"They are so cool!" said Molly.

"Yes, they are," laughed Santa, "and once we have delivered all of the presents, I will let you get better acquainted with every single one of them. So hurry and climb aboard the sleigh and we will be off."

"Okay," said Molly eagerly climbing in beside Santa Claus and snuggling down under the warm mulita-coloured quilts that Mrs. Claus and some of the little elves had made to help keep Santa Claus and his helpers warm during their journey all around the world on this very special evening.

"Lead the way, Rudolf and my faithful reindeer

team," said Santa Claus, "you know where you're going."

"Do Rudolf and the other reindeer's know the whole route without a map?" asked Molly.

"Yes," laughed Santa Claus, "Rudolph leads our team because of his bright red nose, and he wears a special collar that sends him the information. Chuckles, my head elf back home in the North Pole watches our route on the computer screen too. He will be awake until I get back home in the morning making sure that everything works out just fine."

"This is so amazing!" said Molly. "Thank you Santa for letting me come with you."

"You are very welcome," said Santa Claus, "but you are doing me a favour, it is very important that I have help when I deliver the presents, because it makes the journey so much quicker and much, much easier. We are coming up to our first stop, hold on, and prepare for landing!"

Molly put her hands onto the side of the sleigh and held on tight while Rudolf and the reindeers landed on a snowy rooftop.

"Excellent landing, Team," said Santa. "Come along Molly the Elf, you've been up a chimney and now it's time you experienced the fun of going down a chimney. If you thought that going up the chimney was exciting, wait until you get to go down. And now that you have been riding with me for a short while, I think you are ready to be truly a fully-fledged Elf! I will put out the fire in the fire place and then all you need to do is hop in and let the Elf magic do the rest of the work.

"Okay, Santa Claus," said Molly excitedly, "let us do this."

"Here we go," said Santa Claus walking over to the chimney and calling a greeting down it. Molly did not understand what Santa said but before he could ask him,

Santa had gone down the chimney and a moment later, Molly followed suit. She slid down the chimney like it was a banana slide and when she came out in a living room she landed on a cushion that was lovely and soft. When Molly got up, the cushion had magically disappeared!

"Wow, a magic cushion!" said Molly.

"Before the night is over, you will see that there are many magical Christmas things, more than you ever imagined. Now, we need to fill the stockings and set out the presents. You, Molly the Elf, have magic to help get gifts where they need to be. Remember how I flicked my finger at the sack at your house. Everywhere we go, I want you to flick your finger at the sack and then the stockings. I will do it for the Christmas tree. With both of us working, the gifts will come out of my sack twice as fast. Together, we can make up for lost time."

Molly flicked her two fingers at the magical red sack and then pointed it at the four stockings that were hung on the fireplace mantle. Small wrapped gifts flew like magic toward the stockings and within three seconds all of them were filled. Molly looked over at Santa and saw that more gifts had appeared around the Christmas tree.

"Are we done here?" asked Molly.

"Almost," said Santa Claus, "we need to eat the milk and mince pies that the Stevenson children left for us."

"Okay," said Molly, "I wonder where they left the milk and cookies."

"That is the part that we need to perfect at the Pole. We do not have any magical powers when it comes to finding the treats that were left us for. Sometimes, I cannot find the special hiding place and children are disappointed when they find that their hard work was not enjoyed. Come on, you can help me look for them."

Santa Claus and Molly looked in the cupboards and in the fridge and microwave, eventually finding chocolate cookies and apple cider awaiting them on a tray in the oven. It only took a moment for them to finish their treat.

"I have never eaten so fast before," said Molly.

"On Christmas Eve we have special powers which allow us to eat quickly so that we can get going again. Ready, set, up the chimney we go. I will go first, you can follow. All you have to do is step into the fireplace and you will be lifted back to the roof," said Santa Claus.

As Santa Claus flew the sleigh that was drawn by the amazingly athletic reindeer, Molly looked out across the night sky. He looked at the millions of stars that lit up the night sky and at the moon, which was at half. Then, he looked down at all of the trees, houses and buildings below.

"Everything down there is so much smaller from up here," said Molly, "like being in an airplane."

"Yes, it is," said Santa Claus, "it is always interesting to see things from different perspectives. How do you like being an elf so far?"

"It is great," answered Molly, "I never imagined that I would get to help deliver presents on Christmas Eve especially from your flying sleigh with the reindeer."

"You are the first human to ever help me deliver gifts," said Santa Claus, "for being an eight year old boy that is a remarkable accomplishment. I am sorry that Little Elf became ill, but it was fortunate that it happened at the home of someone who was so willing to experience new things to help me out."

"You are welcome, Santa Claus, I am having so much fun," answered Molly. "That is good," said Santa Claus as the sleigh landed on a snowy front lawn.

"Why did we not land on the roof at this house?" asked Molly.

"The Carlson's like many families do not have a chimney

which means that we have to go through the front door," answered Santa Claus.

"But is the door not locked?" asked Molly.

"It probably is that," said Santa Claus, "but we have Christmas magic on our side. Climb on out of the sleigh with me and I will show you. The only difference here is how we get into the house. The rest stays the same."

Together Molly and Santa Claus walked through the snow to the Carlson's front door. It was painted blue and had a Christmas wreath hanging from it. Santa Claus tried to open the door, but just like he and Molly had thought, it was locked, just as it should be. Santa Claus reached into his pocket and pulled out a holly leaf. He set the holly leaf over the keyhole in the door and a second later, the door flew open letting in both Santa and Molly.

"We have a magic holly bush at the North Pole," said Santa Claus, "it is very handy for such occasions and much quicker than trying to pick a lock or having to ring the doorbell waving everyone up inside. The magic holly allows us to get in and out quickly and unnoticed."

"That was so cool," said Molly as he and Santa Claus put out the gifts and filled the stockings for the Carlson children. Then, they found the milk and mince pies and then headed back out the door. Once they were back on the front porch, Santa Claus used his handkerchief to wipe the holly leaf from off the doorknob which locked the door again.

"You think of everything," said Molly excitedly as she and Santa Claus climbed back into the sledge and covered themselves back up with the knitted quilts before preparing for take-off.

"I have a great team at the North Pole, they are always

thinking up fantastic new ideas to make delivering presents as quick and easy as possible. We have to have a lot of magic to travel all over the world in one night," said Santa Claus.

"It was so easy to go through the door," said Molly, "how come you do not use everyone's doors to deliver the gifts to all the boys and girls?"

"That is a good question," said Santa Claus, "I think it is because landing on the roof causes a lot less attention to be drawn to us than if we land in people's yards. When we land in yards, if anyone is awake they might see us. It is not that we do not like seeing people, but that we only have so much time to deliver gifts and we do not want our magical secrets to be revealed."

"That makes sense," answered Molly.

Finally Santa Claus and Molly were almost finished their night. The reindeer had just landed on the top of the last roof. It was at a large orphanage in the middle of a busy city. They headed to the biggest chimney in the place and went down it. Then they got busy. There were no stockings hung on the mantle, and the only Christmas tree that the orphanage had was small but it was decorated with ornaments that the children had made.

"We must go room by room," said Santa Claus, "the children will have left one of their stockings on their bureaus. That is where we will also leave their presents."

Together, Molly and Santa Claus went room by room, quiet

not to wake the sleeping children. Molly filled the stockings and Santa left a nicely wrapped gift. The last room they stopped in belonged to the littlest boy at the orphanage, the boy's name was Howard. Molly filled Howard's stocking, but when Santa Claus flicked his finger at the bag and pointed it at the bureau, nothing happened.

"Oh, oh," said Santa Claus, "we are missing a present. I do not know what happened to it. Elf Molly, can you please go back to the sleigh and see if it fell out and is under the seat?"

"Yes, Santa Claus," answered Molly.

"Thank you," said Santa Claus and he touched Molly's elf costume with one of his fingers. "Now the fire will go out when you go near it. My magic touch will keep you safe."

Molly hurried quietly through the hallway of the orphanage until she got back to the chimney she had slid down before. She entered the fireplace, Santa Claus' magic keeping her safe as she ascended the very large chimney, and back to the roof. Molly then jumped into the back seat of

the sleigh and looked
all around trying to
find the missing gift.
She looked
everywhere, between
the quilts and under
the seat but the
present was nowhere
to be found."

"What will we do?"
said Molly out loud as
she climbed out of
the sleigh and looked
from the chimney to
the reindeer and then
back again. "Howard
must have a present.
Here is here living in

an orphanage. He does not even have presents; he should at least have a happy Christmas. Maybe, Santa Claus will have the answer." Molly went back down the chimney, sliding out on his cushion when he entered the large room that held the fireplace. Once he stood up, the cushion once again disappeared, as it has done at all of the other homes that Molly had visited.

"Did you find the present?" asked Santa Claus meeting Molly.

"No," answered Molly sadly, "Did you?"

"No," replied Santa Claus, "I did not find it. I rechecked each of the children's bedrooms here but it is nowhere to be found. Perhaps it fell out of the sleigh somewhere along our journey. If that happens, the present eventually makes its way back to the North Pole, but sometimes that can take a few days, sometimes even a few weeks if the gift is coming from as far away as Australia."

"So what should we do?" asked Molly, "Howard needs to have a present. I would give him something of mine, but I left my presents under the Christmas tree at my house."

"That is very generous of you, Molly," said Santa Claus, "but we can make a special call to the North Pole and ask them to send us out a special gift. With magic North Pole parcel delivery, it can arrive here in just a few minutes." Santa Claus took out his mobile phone and called the North Pole.

"They are sending us a wooden train set," said Santa Claus,

"would you like to meet it on the roof while I look around for the milk and cookies?"

"Sure," said Molly, and she once again went up the chimney to the rooftop. She was going to sit in the comfortable sleigh to wait for the arrival of the wooden train set, but before she had time to even climb into the sledge, a parcel landed with a gentle thud on the backseat! Molly picked up the package; it was wrapped in green and red paper that had reindeer on it. The gift tag read:

To Howard,
Happy Christmas,
From Santa Claus.

"This is the one," said Molly and she took it back down the chimney with her. Then quietly she carried the present to

Howard's room and set it on the foot of Howard's bed beside his Christmas stocking. Next, she joined Santa Claus for some homemade mince pies and some nice cold milk, before they went back up the chimney.

"Now to take you home, Molly," said Santa Claus, "it's time for you to celebrate Christmas with your family."

"This has been such a wonderful night," said Molly.

"I think so too," said Santa Claus.

Back at Molly's house, the Rudolf and his friends landed on the snow covered roof. It was just beginning to become light outside. Little Elf was waiting for them on the roof. He waved as the sledge landed.

"How are you feeling Little Elf?" asked Santa Claus.

"Much better now," said Little Elf.

"That is good," replied Santa Claus, "We will return to the North Pole soon."

The sledge tracks on the roof from so many hours earlier had already been covered with fresh snow. Molly and Santa Claus climbed out of the sleigh and Little Elf climbed into the back seat and got comfortable under a quilt. As Santa Claus had promised earlier in the night, he introduced Molly to the team of nine reindeer and Molly got the chance to pet each of the reindeer and feed them each a carrot as a reward for their job well done.

"I could not have delivered all of the presents on time

without your help. Thank you, Elf Molly for your help tonight. I need to be getting back to the North Pole now, to celebrate with my family and all of the elves." Then, Santa waved his finger around Molly's head again and once again she was wearing her pink pyjamas. "You have just enough magic to get back down the chimney. The magic cushion will be there for you at the bottom."

Santa peered down the chimney and once again said the magic Christmas words.

"What does that mean, Santa?" asked Molly.

"It's an Elf saying that asks for the flames to be quieted so that magic may intervene."

"That's pretty cool," answered Molly with a smile, "Thank you so much for letting me help you. I will certainly remember this wonderful night forever."

"You are welcome," answered Santa Claus with a warming smile, "Without all of your help, I would not have been able to deliver all of the presents to so many deserving children. You should be very proud of yourself for helping to make so many children happy."

"Thank you, Santa Claus," said Molly as she hopped down the chimney and emerged in her living room on the cushion which promptly disappeared as soon as Molly was standing. She looked around the room seeing her Christmas stocking filled with presents and all the wrapped presents under the Christmas tree. Molly could not wait to see what Santa Claus' workshop elves had made her, but more than anything else Molly felt so happy that she was able to help Santa Claus bring joy to boys and girls all around the world.

It was going to be a wonderful memory that she would hold onto forever, even though she knew that she would not be able to tell her friends at school about it – anyhow, Molly knew that even if she did actually tell them about her evening (which she wouldn't, because she had promised Santa Claus) they would not believe her and think that she had made the story up.

Molly had been on an amazing adventure

with Santa and had also learned the value of giving to others. It was a lesson and a night that she would forever remember.

MERRY CHRISTMAS EVERYONE!

Printed in Great Britain
by Amazon